AFTER BEING STRUCK BY A BOLT OF LIGHTNING AND DOUSED
WITH CHEMICALS, POLICE SCIENTIST BARRY ALLEN BECAME
THE FASTEST MAN ON EARTH ...

# SUPER DC HEROES

# The FLASH

WRITTEN BY
LAURIE SUTTON

ILLUSTRATED BY
DAN SCHOENING,
MIKE DeCARLO, AND
LEE LOUGHRIDGE

# GORILLA WARFARE

**www.raintreepublishers.co.uk**
Visit our website to find out
more information about
Raintree books.

**To order:**
☎ Phone 0845 6044371
🖷 Fax +44 (0) 1865 312263
🖳 Email myorders@raintreepublishers.co.uk

Customers from outside the UK please telephone +44 1865 312262

Raintree is an imprint of Capstone Global Library Limited,
a company incorporated in England and Wales having its
registered office at 7 Pilgrim Street, London, EC4V 6LB
– Registered company number: 6695582

First published by Stone Arch Books in 2011
First published in the United Kingdom in 2012
The moral rights of the proprietor have been asserted.

The Flash and all related characters, names, and elements
are trademarks of DC Comics © 2011.

All rights reserved. No part of this publication may be
reproduced in any form or by any means (including
photocopying or storing it in any medium by electronic means
and whether or not transiently or incidentally to some other
use of this publication) without the written permission of the
copyright owner, except in accordance with the provisions
of the Copyright, Designs and Patents Act 1988 or under the
terms of a licence issued by the Copyright Licensing Agency,
Saffron House, 6–10 Kirby Street, London EC1N 8TS (www.
cla.co.uk). Applications for the copyright owner's written
permission should be addressed to the publisher.

Art Director: Bob Lentz
Designer: Brann Garvey
Production Specialist: Michelle Biedschied
Editor: Vaarunika Dharmapala
Originated by Capstone Global Library Ltd
Printed and bound in China by Leo Paper Products Ltd

ISBN 978 1 406 22716 1 (paperback)
15 14 13 12 11
10 9 8 7 6 5 4 3 2 1

**British Library Cataloguing in Publication Data**
A full catalogue record for this book is available
from the British Library.

# CONTENTS

# CHAPTER 1

# MONKEYS ON MAIN STREET

Police scientist Barry Allen sat in his lab at police headquarters in Central City. He was looking at a scrap of cloth under a powerful microscope.

The fabric was from a crime scene, and his job was to study it for clues. The threads were swollen, which meant they had been soaking in water or in some other liquid. There were many bodies of water in Central City. The fabric could have been in an aquarium, the river, or in someone's swimming pool.

Barry was looking for traces of evidence that would tell him which one of these possibilties was true.

**WHAAAMMMMM!** A police officer burst into the lab.

"Barry! You've got to come and take a look at this!" the officer shouted. "It's the weirdest thing I've ever seen!"

This statement made Barry curious. Central City was the home of the super hero Flash, so strange things happened all the time. If the Mirror Master, the Trickster, or Captain Cold had not escaped, then there was some other super-villain on the loose. They were always trying to beat the local super hero.

Barry Allen knew all of this very well because secretly … he was the Flash!

*Which crook is it this time?* Barry
wondered.

He stepped out of his lab and could not
believe what he saw. Everyone was running
up and down the corridors. People were
yelling. The entire police force was on alert.

"Monkeys!" someone screamed.

"Robots!" shouted someone else.

"It's an army!" an officer yelled.

Barry could see the television in the
station canteen across the corridor. The
local news was on. A reporter stood in front
of an amazing scene. Barry's friend was
right about the situation being the weirdest
thing he had ever seen. An army of robot
monkeys was attacking Central City!

"The robot monkeys appear to have
three distinct forms," the reporter said.

"I've seen a monkey shape, a chimp shape, and a gorilla shape," the reporter continued.

*SMASH!* A giant metal fist pounded the street not far from the reporter. Chunks of asphalt flew into the air. The reporter ran and so did the cameraman. The picture fizzled with static and then went black.

"We switch now to the world news," the news presenter said. "Robots have overtaken all of the world's largest cities! London, Madrid, and New York are all under attack!"

The television showed metal baboons climbing the Eiffel Tower in Paris. Then the picture switched to giant gorilla robots smashing the pyramids in Egypt.

Barry Allen had seen enough.

"This is a job for the Flash!" Barry said.

Barry stepped back into his lab and closed the door. He did not want anyone to see what he did next. Barry touched a secret switch on his special gold ring.

**WHOOOOSH!**

The Flash's red and yellow super hero uniform unfolded from inside the high-tech jewellery. Barry put on the uniform at super-speed.

**ZWWWOOOOMMMM!** The Flash ran out of the police station so fast that no one saw him. He got to the battle zone in seconds. Little metal monkeys were ripping apart cars, buses, and lorries. The people inside them were calling out for help.

"I'll put a stop to this monkey business!" Flash shouted.

In the blink of an eye, Flash grabbed a hundred monkeys by their mechanical tails. He held fifty in one hand and fifty in the other hand. Then he brought both bunches together in a giant crash!

**KA-BOOM!** The robots were smashed into tiny pieces.

The giant gorilla robots were next on the super hero's list. The evil apes were knocking down buildings. Some had cannons for hands and were firing missiles at the town hall. **BOOM! BOOM!**

Flash ran at supersonic speed. He zoomed ahead of the missiles, beat them to their targets, and tossed them back at the gorilla robots. Problem solved.

"Help! Help!" someone yelled as the chaos continued.

Flash looked up and spotted a window cleaner under attack. High above the city streets, a troop of metal chimpanzees were swinging on his scaffolding. The man slipped and fell.

Flash did not slow down. In fact, he ran even faster. **WHOOOOSH!**

The Fastest Man Alive sped straight up the side of the building and grabbed the window cleaner in mid-air.

He carried the man up to the roof and then down the other side of the building. It took less than a second for Flash to get the man to safety behind a line of police.

"Thanks, Flash!" the window cleaner exclaimed. "I thought I was going to die!"

"Not when the Fastest Man Alive is around," a nearby officer said.

"Flash, who do you think is behind this attack?" asked the Central City Chief of Police.

"Only one villain would use robot apes to do his dirty work," Flash replied. "The super-simian ... Gorilla Grodd!"

# CHAPTER 2

# LONDON FALLING

Gorilla Grodd sat in his headquarters watching giant television screens. He could see his robot armies all over the world. Grodd wore a high-tech helmet. It was connected to a huge computer that controlled all the robot primates. He pushed a button to talk to the Flash.

"So you guessed it was me?" Grodd said. "You're pretty smart for a human."

Back in Central City, the Flash heard Grodd's voice. It came from a robot monkey head lying on the ground.

Flash picked up the head and looked at it closely. Its eyes were cameras, and its mouth was a speaker.

"Grodd, I see you're up to your old tricks again," Flash said into the mechanical monkey's head.

"My goal has never changed, Flash," Grodd answered. "I'll wipe all humans off the face of the planet, or die trying!"

"Not if I can do anything about it," Flash replied.

The Scarlet Speedster took off so fast that the robot monkey head twirled like a spinning top. Flash looked like a blur of red to the people watching him. Faster than anyone could count to ten, Flash tore the rest of the robot army apart.

Flash took out every screw, bolt, and wire from the mechanical animals.

"That takes care of Central City," Flash said. "Now I have to save the rest of the world from Grodd's crazy plan."

Flash knew that London was under attack. He had seen the pictures on television. It did not matter that London was on the other side of the Atlantic Ocean. The Flash would have to get there – fast!

An aeroplane took five hours to cross the Atlantic Ocean. A ship took a week to get from one side to the other. The Flash took seconds! He ran across the top of the water, moving so fast that he did not have time to sink.

Reaching the United Kingdom, the first thing Flash saw was the London Eye.

The giant wheel was covered with robot orangutans. They were trying to pull the London Eye right down into the nearby River Thames.

"Not so fast!" Flash shouted at the mad monkeys.

Within an instant, the super hero had grabbed every last robot and thrown them all into the water.

*SPLASH!* Each one sank quickly to the bottom of the river, unable to keep their steel frames afloat.

Flash did not stop to celebrate. He rushed to Buckingham Palace. This building was covered with robot howler monkeys. They were making a terrible sound. *HWOOT! HWOOT! HWOOT!* The noise was shaking the building apart.

"This is not music to my ears," said the Flash.

Then the super hero took off. He ran in circles around the palace until he reached the speed of sound. **KA-BOOM!**

The sonic boom hit the robots and knocked them off the building. They shorted out and hit the ground.

Flash picked up one of the robot heads and looked into its camera eyes. "Grodd, I'm going to put a monkey wrench in your plans," he shouted.

Gorilla Grodd was not paying attention to his television screens. He was not even hooked up to the robot controls. The evil ape was working on a giant satellite dish. He heard what Flash said, but it did not matter to him.

"Flash doesn't know my real plan at all!" Grodd said to himself. "He thinks the robots are all I've got."

Gorilla Grodd laughed. He believed humans were worthless and that simians were superior beings. Grodd had vowed to remove all humans from the face of the planet. This time Grodd had the perfect plan to accomplish his ultimate goal.

"I sent in my robot armies just to keep Flash busy," Grodd continued to boast. "I need time to finish building this DNA Doomsday Device. It will change the DNA of every human on the planet. I'm going to turn the people of Earth into apes!"

So far, Gorilla Grodd's plan was working.

The Flash remained very busy. He zoomed all over London, battling the armies of robot monkeys. He made a super tornado to suck up the robot chimps wrecking the Tower of London. He made ropes out of broken robot monkey tails to keep London Bridge from falling down. When a giant metal gorilla robot climbed to the top of Big Ben, Flash made the robot spin so fast it flew apart.

"Sorry about the mess," Flash told some police officers.

"That's all right, Flash," an officer said. "You've saved us all."

Flash knew that London was only one of the cities in danger. Grodd had sent his armies to all the world's capitals. This was going to be a real test of his super-speed.

# CHAPTER 3

# NO MORE MONSTERS

Flash sped across the English Channel from London to Paris, France. The robot baboons he had seen on television were still clinging to the famous Eiffel Tower.

*FWOOOSHHHHH!!* Flash took care of them with a giant whirlwind.

After he defeated all the robots in the French capital, Flash raced on to Madrid, Spain. Then he went to Berlin in Germany and Oslo in Norway. The super hero zoomed across Europe, battling chimps in Rome, Athens, and Moscow.

Flash ran through many more countries and time zones. It had been daytime in Central City when he left. When he got to Tokyo, Japan, it was night. He was on the other side of the planet from where he had started.

The people of Tokyo were fighting Grodd's metal monkeys. They knew all about monsters and giant robots. But there were too many for the people to fight. The Japanese were losing the battle.

Flash sped all over the city of Tokyo. By now he knew how to deal with the pesky robots. He had had plenty of practice.

Flash turned up the heat on a bunch of robot chimps. He melted them with the friction of his super-fast hands. All that was left was a pile of hot molten metal.

Flash saw some giant robot gorillas firing missiles at the Imperial Palace.

"Let's play tag," Flash said.

He ran up to one of the gorilla robots and tapped it on the shoulder.

"You're it!" Flash said.

Then he ran and tapped another. He ran to a third robot and did the same thing. Soon every gorilla robot was totally confused. They did not know which way to turn. They were so rattled that their circuits blew out. **KA-BOOM!**

The howler monkey robots screeched until the ground shook. The sound was worse than an earthquake. Flash pulled all the wires from their voice control boxes at super-speed. He finished the job by punching them with his fists.

"Silence is golden," Flash said.

At last the battle was over. Flash had beaten all of Grodd's robots, and the human race was safe once again.

"So why isn't Grodd saying anything?" Flash said to himself. "He usually boasts to me that he'll try again."

The speedy super hero picked up a robot head and tried to get Grodd to reply. "Grodd, your robot armies are destroyed," Flash said. "Don't you have anything to say about that?"

Grodd did not answer, and the Flash became suspicious.

"It's not like Grodd to accept defeat quietly," Flash said. "That can only mean there's more to his evil plan."

Flash knew that Gorilla Grodd was controlling the monkey robots from somewhere else. He must have a hidden headquarters. "I'd better find that simian mastermind ... and fast," Flash said.

**WHOOOOSH!**

In a blur, the Speedster assembled bits of the smashed monkey robots to make a new one. It looked like a tiny glider. This was a very special robot. The Flash had changed its controls. Now it would follow its own radio signal and lead him straight to Grodd's hideout.

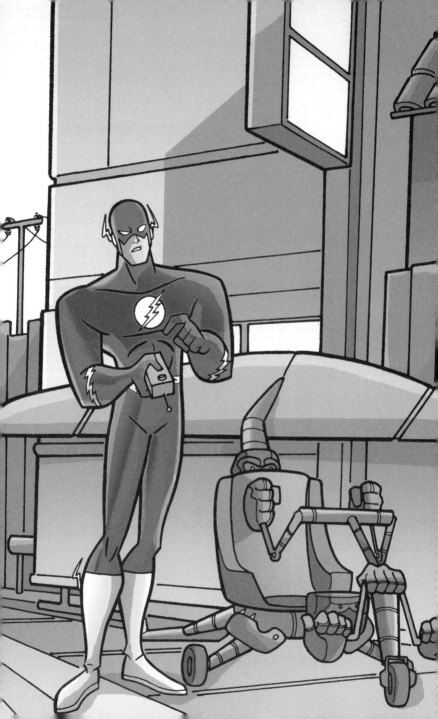

"Ready or not, here I come!" Flash shouted.

The robot glider took off with the Flash on board. It led him away from Tokyo and over the Pacific Ocean.

Suddenly, Flash felt very strange. Something was happening to him. He felt his gloves getting tight. He looked down at his hands and was shocked to see them changing shape. His fingers were getting short and stumpy. His palms were growing wider. Soon, he had chimpanzee hands.

He was turning into an ape!

# CHAPTER 4

# THE FASTEST APE ALIVE

Gorilla Grodd had his hands on the controls of the DNA Device. The machine was on and his plan was in action.

"Every human on Earth will be an ape," Grodd said. "And I will rule them all!"

Grodd watched the giant television screens. Many of the robot eye cameras still worked, and Grodd could see the people in the world's capital cities. They were all slowly changing form. Their arms were growing longer and no one could stand up straight.

Grodd kept a look out for one special human. He searched every centimetre of his high-tech computer maps but could not find him.

"Where is the Flash?" Grodd screamed. "I want to watch him change into the Fastest *Ape* Alive!"

Grodd could not find Flash because he was not in any of the capital cities. He was racing across the Pacific Ocean. The flying monkey glider was leading him to Grodd's secret headquarters.

Unfortunately, just like every other human, Flash was slowly turning into an ape. That did not stop his super-speed. The only difference was now he ran like a super-fast chimp.

Finally, Flash saw land in the distance.

He spotted an island with rows and rows of statues, which looked like giant heads. Flash realized the robot plane was heading straight for Easter Island.

"So this is where you're hiding, Grodd," Flash said to himself.

Easter Island was made up of three extinct volcanoes. The robot glider flew Flash to one of the craters, which was perfectly round and had a lake in the middle. It looked like a giant stone bowl.

Flash jumped from the glider on to the ground below. **CRASH!** The robot glider crashed into the side of the crater. He looked closer at the crash site and saw a steel door. It was hidden behind thick rock.

*This must be Grodd's front door,* Flash thought. *I think I'll just let myself in.*

**WHIR-WHIR-WHIR-WHIR!**

Flash began to vibrate. When he did this fast enough, he could pass through solid objects. The super hero took a step towards the steel door.

**THUD!** He bounced off the steel. "I didn't expect that!" Flash said. "Grodd must have used super-strong metal."

Flash whirled his hands in super-fast circles to make twin tornadoes. The strong winds tore off the rocks, but not the door.

"My super-speed doesn't work on this door," Flash said. "Grodd must have known I'd show up."

Flash had to get inside Grodd's hideout. Whatever was turning humans into apes was in there. And the Scarlet Speedster was looking more like a chimp every minute!

Grodd had put up some special defences against super-speed. How was Flash going to get past them?

*There's only one thing left to do,* Flash thought. *If I can't use super-speed to get in there, then I won't use quickness at all.*

Flash stood very still and studied the door carefully. It looked like the entrance to a bank vault. There were latches and gear wheels on it. All the parts fitted together like the inside of a watch.

For most people, the vault would have looked like a complex puzzle. However, as a police scientist, Barry had been trained in the art of picking locks. He reached out and slowly lifted a tiny latch. All the gears turned and the wheels spun. Other latches popped. The big steel door unlocked, and Flash quickly pulled it open.

On the other side of the door was a long tunnel. Flash knew the passage had to lead to Grodd's hidden base. He decided to take it slow. If there were speed defences on the door, maybe Grodd had booby-trapped the tunnel as well.

Flash wanted to run. The clock was ticking on humanity, and the countdown was almost at zero. His own body was showing him how close it was to the end. He was hunched over and walking on his knuckles. The super hero could feel the shape of his jaw changing. His ears were getting larger.

At last, he came to the end of the tunnel, which opened into a huge cave. In the middle of the secret laboratory stood the evil ape himself, Gorilla Grodd. He was standing in front of a high-tech machine.

On top of the machine was a giant satellite dish. Flash knew this device was responsible for turning people into apes.

The Scarlet Speedster had to stop it!

# CHAPTER 5

# TOP BANANA

With no time to spare, Flash raced across the lab towards the super-villain.

Stun beams shot out of the ceiling and walls, triggered by his super-speed. Flash was not surprised.

*Leave it to Grodd to have speed defences in here too*, he thought. The super hero tried to dodge the beams but was clumsy in his new ape form. His legs did not work the way they used to.

Flash stopped trying to run. Instead, he leapt into the air, grabbed one of the hanging stun guns and swung like a monkey. He climbed around and around the cave lab.

That got Grodd's attention. "Flash! How clever of you to find my headquarters," Grodd said. "What do you think of my latest project?"

"I don't … *hoo hoo* … like it … *eee eee* … at all!" Flash said.

The super hero's voice was changing, too. His vocal cords were turning into a chimpanzee's. Soon he would be unable to talk.

"I'm making the world a better place," Grodd said. "Humans have made such a mess of this planet."

"You're not doing this for the world," Flash answered. "You're doing this … *hoo hoo* … for your own selfish reasons."

"The human rule on Earth is over," Grodd shouted. "It's time for the reign of King Grodd!"

Flash did not dare slow down. One hit from the stun beams, and he would be finished. The speedster had to think of a way out of this trap – while he could still think. His brain was changing along with the rest of his body.

Flash grabbed one of the stun guns. Instead of swinging on it, he used it to shoot the other stun guns.

As fast as Grodd could blink, Flash knocked out the speed defences.

"Don't crown yourself … *eee eee* … king of the world yet, Grodd," Flash said.

It took less than a second for Flash to reach the DNA Device. He studied the complex controls. It would take some time to work them out. Humanity did not have that time.

Flash raised a vibrating fist. He was ready to smash the machine into bits.

"I wouldn't do that if I were you," Grodd said. "If you destroy the DNA Device there's no reversing its effects. People will remain apes forever!"

"Tell me … *hoo hoo* … how to turn this thing off," Flash demanded.

"No," Grodd said. "I think I'll turn you off instead."

Flash felt his mind go fuzzy.

Then all of a sudden, Flash could not remember where he was or what he was doing. Something was very wrong. Flash could not even run. He was frozen!

"The human brain is so easy to control," Grodd said. "It's no match for my telepathy crown!" He pointed at the gleaming helmet on top of his head.

Grodd had used his mind control abilities to stop Flash in his tracks. The super hero was now helpless.

"There's no stopping the final phase," Grodd said, pointing at a row of monitors. "Watch those television screens."

Flash had no choice but to obey. He saw the people he had rescued from Grodd's armies of robots take on the final shapes of chimpanzees, gorillas, and orangutans.

Something was happening to Flash. His mind was clearing! He could think for himself again. The DNA Device only controlled humans, not apes. The closer Flash got to being an ape, the less mind control Grodd had on him. Flash knew he had to act now, or he would lose his humanity forever.

**KA-POW!** Flash gave Grodd a super-fast punch. Grodd never saw it coming. One second, he had Flash helpless, and the next he was seeing stars.

Flash knew there was only one way to stop the DNA Device without destroying it. He had to make it short-circuit. He had to give it so much electricity that it would shut itself off.

Flash turned himself into a turbine. He whirled like a wheel in a generator.

The friction he created caused sparks. Then the sparks turned into a giant lightning bolt! The nearest metal object attracted the bolt. ZZRRRRTT!

The DNA Device surged with electricity. All the safety switches tripped. So did all the switches in the lab. The whole cave suddenly went dark!

"That's what I call one big off-switch," Flash said with a smile.

It took a while for Flash to get the lights back on, but he was not in a hurry anymore. He could take his time reversing the DNA Device. He had found Grodd's blueprints.

He quickly tied up Gorilla Grodd. Still, Flash knew he had to find somewhere secure to put the simian super-genius.

\*    \*    \*

When Grodd woke up from his knockout blow, he was in jail. It was a very special jail. The bars were made from the smashed pieces of his monkey robot army! The guards were re-programmed gorilla robots. The DNA Device and the lab machines were gone.

"Do you like what I've done with the place?" Flash asked, now human again.

"You beat me this time, Flash!" Grodd said, "but I'll succeed one day!"

"You always say that," Flash replied. "Why can't you learn you'll never be top banana with me around?"

File  Edit  View  Go  Window  Help

○ ○ ○       GORILLA GRODD

# GORILLA GRODD

**REAL NAME: GRODD**

**OCCUPATION: WORLD CONQUEROR**

**HEIGHT: 2 METRES**

**WEIGHT: 272 KILOGRAMS**

**EYES: GREY**

**HAIR: GREY**

**SPECIAL POWERS/ABILITIES:**

Telepathy (the ability to read people's minds); telekinesis (being able to move objects by thought alone); genius scientist and inventor; super-strength.

done

GORILLA GRODD BIO

**BIOGRAPHY:**

A race of super-intelligent apes live in the deepest jungles of Africa. Known as Gorilla City, the kingdom is populated with kind and noble apes. However, one of them, Gorilla Grodd, has sinister plans for the highly evolved primates. He wants to conquer Earth and enslave humanity! When his fellow primates refused to follow, Solovar, the apes' leader, contacted the Flash via telepathy for help. The Scarlet Speedster was able to stop Grodd's scheme, but the ape still runs wild.

GORILLA GRODD EXTRAS

Grodd has made no fewer than eighteen attempts to destroy all human life on Earth.

Despite being an ape, Grodd has a genius-level understanding of science and technology.

Grodd possesses a device that lets him control the minds of others. Approach him with caution.

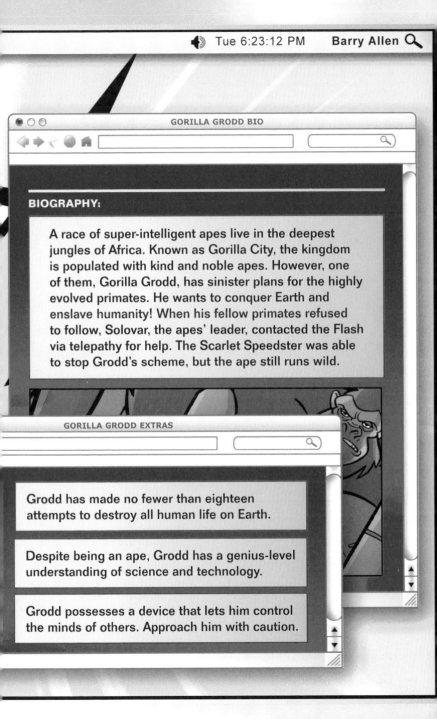

# BIOGRAPHIES

**Laurie Sutton** has read comics since she was a child. She grew up to become an editor for Marvel, DC Comics, Starblaze, and Tekno Comics. She has written *Adam Strange* for DC, *Star Trek: Voyager* for Marvel, as well as *Star Trek: Deep Space Nine* and *Witch Hunter* for Malibu Comics. There are long boxes of comics in her wardrobe where there should be clothes and shoes. Laurie has lived all over the world.

From an early age, **Dan Schoening** has had a passion for animation and comic books. Dan currently does freelance work in the animation and games industry and spends a lot of time with his lovely little daughter, Paige.

**Mike DeCarlo** is a long-term contributor of comic art whose range extends from Batman and Iron Man to Bugs Bunny and Scooby-Doo. He lives with his wife and four children.

**Lee Loughridge** has been working in comics for more than fifteen years. He currently lives in a tent on the beach.

# GLOSSARY

**DNA** molecule that carries the genetic code which gives living things their special characteristics

**extinct** if a volcano is extinct, it has stopped erupting

**humanity** being a human; the human race

**molten** melted by heat

**primate** any member of the group of animals that includes humans, apes, and monkeys

**satellite** spacecraft that is sent into orbit around Earth, the Moon, or another planet

**scaffolding** wooden planks and metal poles on the outside of a building, used while building, repairing, or cleaning

**simian** resembling monkeys or apes

**sonic boom** noise made by an object travelling faster than the speed of sound

**telepathy** communication with another person using only the mind

# DISCUSSION QUESTIONS

1. The Flash has super-speed. Gorilla Grodd has super-strength. Which superpower would you rather have? Why?

2. Why do you think Grodd wanted the rest of the world to be just like him? Would you want everyone to be just like you? Why or why not?

3. Of the ten illustrations in this book, which one is your favourite? Why?

# WRITING PROMPTS

1. Write another chapter to this book where Grodd escapes his metal cage. How does the Flash handle the simian super-villain? Write about it.

2. Create your own super hero. What superpowers does he or she have? What weaknesses? What does his or her costume look like? Write about your new super hero.

3. Imagine that you are being turned into an animal. What type of animal would you want to become? Write about your transformation. Then draw a picture of your animal self!

# MORE NEW

# FLASH

# ADVENTURES!

WRATH OF THE
WEATHER WIZARD

ATTACK OF
PROFESSOR ZOOM!

SHADOW OF THE SUN

CAPTAIN COLD'S
ARCTIC ERUPTION

SHELL SHOCKER